For my son, Thomas Ellinas — G. E.

For Caz Royds — J. R.

First U.S. edition 2020
First published by Walker Books (U.K.) 2019

Library of Congress Catalog Card Number pending
ISBN 978-1-5362-1144-3

20 21 22 23 24 25 CCP 10 9 8 7 6 5 4 3 2 1

Printed in Shenzhen, Guangdong, China

This book was typeset in Filosofia.
The illustrations were done in watercolor.

Candlewick Press
99 Dover Street
Somerville, Massachusetts 02144

visit us at www.candlewick.com

CANDLEWICK PRESS

SHAKESPEARE'S
GLOBE

WILLIAM SHAKESPEARE

The Tempest

retold by Georghia Ellinas

illustrated by Jane Ray

Can you do magic?

I am Ariel, a spirit of the air. I can fly, ride on
the curled clouds, and burn bright as fire.
Magic is in every part of me.

My noble master, Prospero, is a clever magician.
This story is about how my master and I used magic
to do strange, frightening, yet brilliant things.

Prospero was the duke of Milan. Since he's a man, not a spirit like me, he had to read special books on how to make magic.

He spent so long in his library that he did not see that his jealous brother, Antonio, wanted to become the duke. Alonso, the ambitious king of Naples, and his brother, Sebastian, plotted with Antonio to overthrow Prospero and his baby daughter, Miranda.

One dark and windy night, Antonio bundled them into a
leaky boat and cast them out on the waters to an unknown fate.

A kind friend had hidden food, water, and Prospero's books
in the boat, because he knew they were too important
to leave behind.

The boat drifted onto the shores of this beautiful island, which is full of sounds and sweet delights. But the island hasn't always been this way. Before Prospero was washed ashore, an evil witch, Sycorax, and her monstrous son, Caliban, had ruled it.

Life was hard for me then. Sycorax hated me and
imprisoned me in a hollow tree for twelve long years.
Thankfully, Prospero heard my desperate crying and
released me from my prison.

But my freedom had a price.
Now, I had to use my magic
to serve Prospero.

For many years I served my master faithfully. But Caliban still thought the island belonged to him. He hated us and wanted us to leave, so Prospero made him chop and carry wood as punishment.

I watched Miranda grow into a beautiful young woman.
She loved her father dearly, but she must
have been lonely sometimes.

One day, Prospero said that he had an important job for me.
His wicked brother, Antonio, was sailing past the island.
On board the ship were Alonso, the king of Naples, and his brother,
Sebastian. Alonso's son, Prince Ferdinand, who knew nothing
of his father's wrongdoing, was also with them.

This was Prospero's only chance to punish the men who
had stolen his dukedom. My master said that if I helped
him get his revenge, he would set me free.

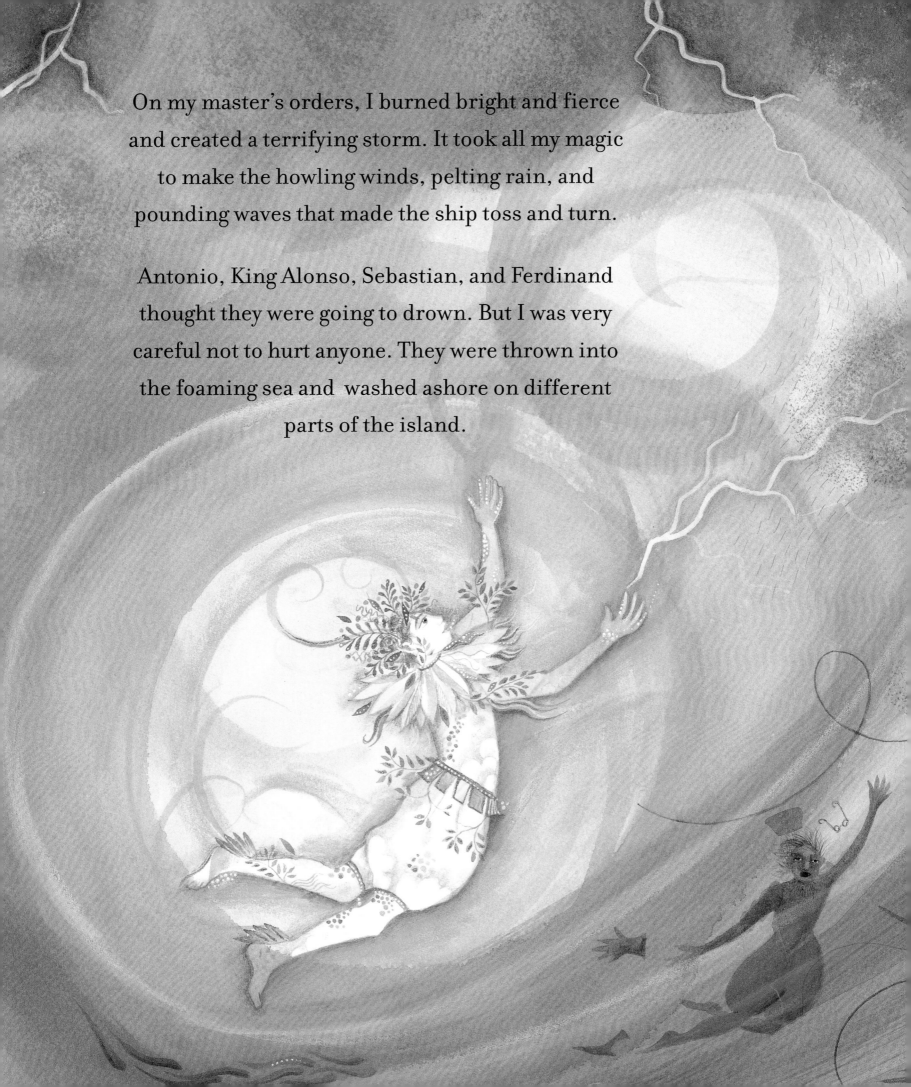

On my master's orders, I burned bright and fierce
and created a terrifying storm. It took all my magic
to make the howling winds, pelting rain, and
pounding waves that made the ship toss and turn.

Antonio, King Alonso, Sebastian, and Ferdinand
thought they were going to drown. But I was very
careful not to hurt anyone. They were thrown into
the foaming sea and washed ashore on different
parts of the island.

Prospero wanted King Alonso to think that his son had drowned. I was sad to see Alonso crying for his lost son and Ferdinand crying for his lost father, but I knew not to question my master. He had a very quick temper, and I didn't want to go back into that hollow tree again!

Full fathom five thy father lies; Of his bones are coral made; Those are pearls that were his eyes: Nothing of him that doth fade

I sang a song about Alonso to cast a spell on Ferdinand and brought him to Prospero. The best way to cast a spell is to sing it. My singing has calmed the angriest animal. I sung to Ferdinand about his father. This magic was easy after making the tempest.

But doth suffer a sea-change Into something rich and strange. Sea-nymphs hourly ring his knell Hark! Now I hear them, Ding-dong, bell.

At my master's command, I broke the spell and
Ferdinand opened his eyes. The first person
he saw was Miranda gazing at him in great
surprise. Ferdinand thought she
was a goddess.

In that moment, they fell in love.

Prospero's plan was working.

I spent the rest of the day doing my
master's bidding: I chased Caliban through the
forest because he had been up to no good—again;
I terrified my master's enemies, creating a feast
that vanished when anyone touched the food; and
I even became a horrible creature and reminded
Antonio of the wrong he and King Alonso had done
to Prospero. I was here, there, and everywhere.
But soon I would get my reward.

Prospero then commanded that I bring Antonio, King Alonso, and Sebastian to his cave. My master used his staff to create a magic circle from which they could not escape.

They could not move or speak, but they could hear every word he said. This was my master's moment for revenge.

Prospero rebuked
them for their cruel
crimes. He demanded
that the disloyal Antonio
give him the dukedom back.
Prospero had the power
to destroy them.

I had to say something
to stop Prospero. I told
him that if I were a mortal,
I would forgive them.

My master thought for a long time, and even though
it was hard, he forgave them. He showed that he had more
kindness in him than they had in them. He even forgave
Caliban and gave him back his island.

King Alonso was still sad because he believed his son was gone.
But Prospero then revealed Ferdinand with Miranda.
Miranda was to marry Ferdinand and
become queen of Naples.

Prospero showed that forgiveness
is greater than revenge. And from
that day he gave up magic forever.
He broke his magic staff into pieces
and drowned his books in the deep
sea. Then Prospero was free to leave
the island and return to his home as
the rightful duke of Milan.

And then he set me free!

Where the bee sucks, there suck I:
In a cowslip's bell I lie;
There I couch when owls do cry.
On the bat's back I do fly
After summer merrily.
Merrily, merrily shall I live now
Under the blossom that hangs on the bough.

We are such stuff

As dreams are made on, and our little life

Is rounded with a sleep.

Prospero, Act 4, Scene 1